Text copyright © Anthony Masters 1999
Illustrations copyright © Alan Marks 1999

First published in Great Britain in 1999
by Macdonald Young Books

Re-issued in 2008 by Wayland

Printed in China

British Library Cataloguing in Publication Data available

ISBN: 978 0 7502 5412 0

Wayland is a division of Hachette Children's Books,
an Hachette Livre UK Company
www.hachettelivre.co.uk

The Curse of
the Frozen Loch

ANTHONY MASTERS

Illustrated by Alan Marks

WAYLAND

Chapter One

An icy wind howled through the cottage, and Will woke up, knowing that something was wrong.

Running into his sister's bedroom, Will found Sarah standing by the window.

"She's out there." Sarah's voice shook.

"Who is?" asked Will.

"Great-Aunt Fiona. She's out on the loch."

Pulling on coats and boots over their pyjamas, they hurried downstairs, only to find the back door swinging wide open.

Outside, the searing cold seemed to reach inside them, like clutching, icy fingers.

"Wait a minute," muttered Will.

"What is it?" asked Sarah.

"There's someone skating."

Sarah gasped. Crackling hoar frost lit a figure with long skirts in the centre of the loch who was skating in increasingly wide arcs. Worse still, Great-Aunt Fiona was walking slowly across the ice towards her, slipping and sliding as she went.

Now, Will and Sarah were on the frozen
loch themselves, the piercing wind biting
into them.

Suddenly, there was the terrible sound of
cracking ice, and in the blue-white light they
watched helplessly as a huge hole widened in
front of the skating figure. Seconds later she
fell into the freezing dark water.

Great-Aunt Fiona was a few metres away
from them now, staring ahead, her eyes
blank, as if she were in a trance.

"Come on," yelled Sarah. "We've got to
get her."

Panting hard, Sarah caught up with Great-Aunt Fiona and, grabbing her arms, began to steer her back to the warm, golden lights of her cottage on the shore. She didn't resist, and Sarah soon found that she was almost carrying her.

"Take her inside," said Will. "I won't be long."

"Where are you going?"
Sarah asked fearfully.

"I've got to try and save
the skater."

"You're not going back
on the ice?"

But Will had already darted
away before his sister could stop him,
running along the shores of the loch until
he was opposite the hole through which
the mystery skater had plunged.

"Come back," yelled Sarah, her voice buffeted by the steely wind.

But Will was sliding about on the glittering black ice.

Shivering so much he could hardly stand, he took small, terrified steps, but the surface now seemed solid and unbroken and he couldn't find the slightest sign of a hole.

The wind whistled and the cold intensified. Suddenly Will was even more afraid, sure the ice would crack at any moment and the deadly waters of the loch would take him just like the skater.

He began to run back towards the shore, his heart pounding, feet sliding, but miraculously. still managing to keep his balance.

Chapter Two

"You stupid idiot! You could have drowned out there." Sarah hissed at him when Will, now crouched over the blazing fire, told his sister what he had seen.

"It's as if it never happened. I just don't understand it. Who was that figure?"

"I don't know," replied Sarah. "But Great-Aunt Fiona doesn't seem much the worse for wear – and that's a real miracle."

Sure enough, the old lady was half asleep in her rocking chair by the fire, a cup of tea in one bony hand.

Will and Sarah had only arrived yesterday at their great-aunt's remote cottage in the Scottish Highlands. They had often been to stay with her before, but this time she had not been her usual warm and friendly self. Instead, Great-Aunt Fiona had been quiet and withdrawn, always gazing uneasily out of the window, staring at the frozen loch.

Sarah heard her mother's voice ringing in her ears. "I honestly don't think Fiona should go on living on her own in that wilderness. Maybe sheltered housing's the only answer."

But Sarah and Will had always admired Great-Aunt Fiona's independence and her love of the wild, lonely landscape.

Now, as they sat in the firelight, Sarah decided to try and break into their great-aunt's strange mood.

"Why were you out on the ice?"

"Are you mad?" The old lady was immediately indignant.

"But we rescued you..."

Great-Aunt Fiona eyed them both with increasing dismay. "I don't know what you're talking about. You were very silly to go out there on a night like this. What on earth would your parents think?"

Will began to protest, but she only became even more angry with them.

Eventually they calmed Great-Aunt Fiona and persuaded her to go to bed. When she had gone, Will said, "Do you think she's gone crazy?"

"I don't know." Sarah sounded worried. "We've got to watch her. Night and day."

Will woke to a chanting sound, but he couldn't make out the words. He was freezing cold and when he went into Sarah's room he could see she was sitting up in bed.

"Let's go and see if she's all right," she said.

In Great-Aunt Fiona's room, Will and Sarah found her with her window wide open, blasts of cold air streaming inside as she gazed out at the loch.

The old lady turned back to them. Her eyes stared right through them as she began to chant again:

> *"If the loch you skate,*
> *The curse you'll break.*
> *If you leave well alone,*
> *Her ghost will always roam."*

"What do you mean?" whispered Sarah. "We don't understand what you're talking about."

But Great-Aunt Fiona didn't reply, and taking her cold arm, Will gently led her back to bed while Sarah closed the window. A full moon had risen and the ice seemed to glint wickedly up at her. Hurriedly, she drew the curtains.

Chapter Three

Next morning was even colder and the loch was frozen solid.

Although she was silent at breakfast, Great-Aunt Fiona seemed none the worse for her walk on the ice.

Will and Sarah went down to the shore, watching ravens gather just where they had seen the skating figure disappear. As they got nearer, the birds rose in a dark cloud, making their rasping cry, flying towards the gaunt ruins of what looked like an old and abandoned village.

"The loch feels evil," said Will.

"That's just because Great-Aunt Fiona's ill," replied Sarah. "I've been thinking – shouldn't we call Mum and get her to come up and see for herself?"

"She'll only put her in hospital," said Will, "and that's not the point."

"What is the point then?"

"We've got to find out who that skater is."

"We've got to find out what she wants, more likely," said Sarah. "I don't think she's human, do you?"

After lunch, snow began to fall, and to Will and Sarah's relief the stark blackness of the ice was softened.

Great-Aunt Fiona seemed to share their relief, and as the three of them sat round the fire she suddenly seemed to be more like her old self again.

"Did you see that skater?" she asked, and Will and Sarah started. But the old lady didn't wait for a reply. "I've been seeing her every night."

"Why?" Sarah managed to blurt out.

Great-Aunt Fiona replied quite calmly, as if she was talking about something very matter-of-fact. "It's all to do with my ancestor, Morag. There used to be a village on the other side of the loch called Kilta, but it's all in ruins now." She paused, and then added hesitantly, "The villagers thought Morag was a witch."

"And was she?" asked Sarah.

"She was different, that's all. People don't like that – even nowadays. Anyway, the villagers punished Morag by pushing her out on the frozen loch and not letting her come ashore. When the ice melted, she drowned."

Again Great-Aunt Fiona paused as Will and Sarah gazed at her in mounting horror.

"As the freezing waters took her, Morag cursed the loch, promising that each time it froze solid she would put one of the locals into a trance, entice them out on to the ice and drown them."

"I don't remember the water being completely frozen over before," said Will nervously. "Do you?"

"Not for a long time. It must be twenty years since the last person drowned. Revenge is a terrible thing."

Will glanced at Sarah and she knew what he was thinking. Should they warn Great-Aunt Fiona again that Morag had drawn her out on to the ice in a trance?

"No," she hissed at him. "She'd never believe us. But Morag's got to be stopped," said Sarah. "And it's up to us to think of a way of stopping her."

Chapter Four

That night Sarah and Will were determined to stay awake and guard Great-Aunt Fiona. They opened the window in Sarah's room and kept watch.

After what seemed a very long time, the ice on the loch began to glow and the skater slowly and hazily appeared.

"Look at that," whispered Will.

Almost at the same time, a shadowy crowd gathered along the shores of the loch, and as the figure skated towards them the crowd surged forward.

"They won't let poor Morag off the ice."
Sarah had tears in her eyes.

"It'll be poor Great-Aunt Fiona next
unless we can keep her safe," said Will
anxiously. "I keep feeling I'm going to
doze off."

"So do I," said Sarah.

Then Will had an idea. Finding some string in a kitchen drawer, he tied a length across Great-Aunt Fiona's open door and looped it round one of the legs of a hall cupboard. Then he tied the end round his wrist. "I'll wake up immediately if she tries to get out."

"You're more likely to trip her up."
"Better than letting her drown."

Will jerked awake and discovered the string around his wrist had gone loose.

Jumping out of bed, calling Sarah, panic surging, he ran to Great-Aunt Fiona's door only to find the string neatly untied. She was nowhere to be seen.

Meanwhile, Sarah had hurried to her window. Great-Aunt Fiona was briskly striding towards the skating figure, arms outstretched.

"Will!" Sarah yelled desperately. "Will!"

The wind seemed to get inside them again as they raced over the ice towards Great-Aunt Fiona.

As Will and Sarah grabbed Fiona's hands, the skating figure suddenly vanished, and the old lady chanted, "*If the loch you skate, the curse you'll break.*"

Suddenly, Sarah realized the importance of the words. The curse *could* be broken. But only if the loch was skated by someone who *chose* to skate, was brave enough to go on the ice of their own free will.

Sarah shivered. It would be a terrible risk. But Morag had been a good person once. Was she capable of being good again?

"What are you going to do?" asked Will, looking at Sarah suspiciously.

"I'm going to try and break the curse. If I don't, Great-Aunt Fiona will never be safe now that Morag's chosen her," said Sarah.

"You're not going anywhere without me."

"I'm the better skater, Will."

They gazed despairingly at each other until Great-Aunt Fiona began to shiver so violently that Will and Sarah knew they would have to get her back inside the cottage as fast as they could.

Once they had put the old lady to bed, Sarah got her skates and hurried outside, followed by Will.

They gazed at the ice which once again had a steely, wicked glitter.

"I'd better get going," said Sarah miserably.

"I'll be on the shore," Will promised. "If anything goes wrong, I can be out there in seconds."

Will watched anxiously as his sister began to skate on the frozen loch, but there was no sign of Morag.

Then, as Sarah began to circle towards the centre, the wind suddenly dropped and the atmosphere was warmer. How could that happen so quickly? Will wondered, and then a wave of fear swept over him.

Morag had sprung a trap.

Sarah was also surprised by the unexpected change in temperature. One moment the loch had been freezing cold, the next a gust of warm air was blowing in her face.

She skated on, but there was still no sign of Morag. Sarah gazed back at the reassuring figure of her brother on the shore. She waved, and Will waved back.

Then Sarah saw her.

Morag was skating towards Sarah, a small, slight figure, with a look of pleading in her eyes. Morag grabbed at Sarah's hand. She cried out in pain – it was as if she were holding a block of ice.

As they began to skate together, Sarah could see the shadowy crowd on the shores, but worst of all she had lost sight of Will.

Suddenly, without warning, she heard a cracking sound and lost Morag's icy grip. Sarah watched her spiralling out of control, heading for an ever-widening hole.

Chapter Five

Will could see that the ice was beginning to break up. Without thinking of any danger to himself he began to slip and slide across the surface of the loch towards Sarah, who had come to a terrified halt.

"We've got to get back. The ice is melting," Will shouted, pulling her towards the shore, but she resisted him.

"It's no good," cried Sarah. "They won't let us off the loch."

Will turned to stare at the shore, only to see the shadowy crowd lining the banks like shifting fog.

"Don't worry about them," he tried to reassure her. "They can't harm us."

But as he spoke the ice cracked and cracked again, and Will saw a sheet of dark water opening up in front of them.

"Please, Morag," whispered Sarah. "Please don't let us drown. You've got to help us. You've *got* to."

"She is," said Will in amazement. "Just look at that."

A strip of ice was re-forming, providing a path to the shore where the ghostly crowd jostled, waiting for them.

Wings beat above them and they cried out in fear as the ravens flew low over their heads.

"We've got to move," cried Will, "like now!"

The ice path was so narrow that they had to walk in single-file, while the ravens made their harsh cries.

The ghostly crowd surged forward and Sarah hesitated.

"Keep going," breathed Will. "They can't stop us."

But suddenly it was as if they had hit a dense patch of fog which clawed at their throats and eyes and ears, long fingers dipping down into their lungs, making them choke and wheeze.

Just as Will and Sarah thought their lungs were going to burst, the foggy mass fell apart in strands. Then they felt their feet strike hard ground and breathed in the glorious fresh air.

Sarah took off her skates and they ran
to the cottage door. All the windows were
ablaze with welcoming light and there was a
delicious smell of hot soup and baking bread.

When Will opened the back door that led
into the kitchen, Great-Aunt Fiona was once
more back to her old self.

"A midnight skate," she said, "deserves
a midnight feast." She seemed to have no
memory of what had happened.

Sarah and Will hurriedly locked the door
behind them.

Later, they sleepily opened the bedroom window and gazed out over the loch. The night was still, the frost had gone and so had the wicked glitter of the ice.

"Is Morag at peace?" asked Will.

"I think so," said Sarah. "She rescued us, and that must have broken the curse. Morag has proved she was a good person – despite what the villagers did to her."

A bird flew low over the water and then past their bedroom window.

For a moment they stared into the raven's glittering eyes. Then it flew silently away.

DARE TO BE SCARED!

*Are you brave enough to try more titles in the Tremors series?
They're guaranteed to chill your spine…*

The Curse of the Ghost Horse by Anthony Masters
Only Jake believes the eerie tale of Black Bess, a handsome black
mare that fell to her death when she was forced to jump a huge
crevasse. From that day, bad luck and Black Bess's ghost have
haunted the area. Tormented by his father's illness, Jake is
determined to jump the crevasse and find Black Bess. But will
Jake's obsession lead to his death?

The Headmaster's Ghost by Sam Godwin
It's the school trip to Mortimer Hall. Adam and Melissa decide to
scare Danny senseless by telling him the story of the evil
headmaster's ghost who haunts the house. Danny is determined
to show he isn't scared. But does his detemination bring him
more than he bargained for…?

Terror in the Attic by Barbara Mitchrlhill
A lodger has rented the attic in Craig and Kelly's house, but there
is something odd about him. Why does he always dress in black?
What is in his leather bag? Desperate to solve the mystery of this
stranger they decide to explore the attic. But does their curiosity
get the better of them…?

*All these books and many more can be purchased from your local
bookseller. For more information about Tremors, write to:
The Sales Department, Hachette Children's Books,
338 Euston Road, London NW1 3BH.*